Mitsuaki

Iwago's

Kangaroos

Mitsuaki Iwago

CHRONICLE BOOKS

SAN FRANCISCO

In 1986, anticipating Australia's bicentennial in 1988, Mitsuaki Iwago traveled to Australia in order to photograph the wild animals of the land Down Under. Impressed by the vastness of the outback—a vastness sharply brought home to this Tokyo resident when he saw a sign announcing that the next gas station was 500 miles away—and impressed by the red kangaroo, Iwago returned to Australia in 1990 specifically to photograph this marvelous animal. The photographs that follow are a result of the two trips, and they provide a spectacular look at the magnificent red kangaroo and the Australian outback.

In the early morning chill, the spirit of these male red kangaroos is at its peak.

A flock of parrots darts into the sky
as a red kangaroo arrives at a creek to drink.

Across the western horizon, rain falls, coloring
the sky slate blue.

The first morning light pours over the red earth.

A large red kangaroo can propel itself forward about thirty-three feet in a single jump.

A baby kangaroo, called a "joey," will stay inside its mother's pouch for about 230 days.

Then, for a time, it will venture out, returning regularly to the pouch. Once the joey is too large

to fit comfortably in its mother's pouch she will rebuff it, and the young kangaroo will not

try to climb in again. Although they are no longer welcome in the pouch, until they are ready to

become independent, joeys will continue to stay near their mothers.

The temperature rises rapidly after 9:00 a.m. Here, a male kangaroo seeks out the shade of a tree.

In the high grass that stretches out across the horizon, I encounter a male red kangaroo. He is standing straight-up on his hind legs, as much as six-and-a-half feet tall. He looks like a human being standing out in the middle of the desert, bearing an air of perfect composure. Fooled by his humanlike stance, I almost ask myself why someone is standing in this deserted place.

During the summer (from November to February), the outback is hot and dry. Often, the temperature rises above 100° Fahrenheit and occasionally hits 120° Fahrenheit. Feeling dull from the heat, I can only watch the red kangaroo from within my roasting vehicle.

In such extreme conditions, the kangaroo himself must feel hot. He constantly licks his forepaws, moistening them over and over in order to cool his body down through evaporation. No other kangaroos are around. After a while, he slowly squats down and begins to eat the grass, which is hard and dry and appears to be stiff in his mouth. He strips the grass off with his forepaws and eats it, every so often scratching here and there around his body.

As I stare at this kangaroo, I notice that his big ears, shoulder muscles, short forepaws, long hind legs, and thick tail alter smoothly and slowly along with his movements. Those shapes, which look so out of balance for a mammal, evolved one by one as the red kangaroo adapted to living in this harsh desert.

Suddenly, I realize that I am facing him over a surprisingly short distance. He is right in front of me. Although he knows the car is approaching, he keeps on eating and scratching. Without realizing it, I have slipped into the relaxed atmosphere of the kangaroo's rhythm.

At the water hole these kangaroos take their time drinking their fill.

At the water's edge, the kangaroos are on their guard, ready to react to any slight sound or movement.

After a meal of grass, this kangaroo hiccups,
causing its entire body to rock back and forth.

While leaping, a kangaroo changes direction by sharply striking the ground with its tail.

The kangaroo's heavy and powerful tail
helps it to keep its balance.

The only large mammals to hop, kangaroos can move at twelve to fifteen miles per hour, accelerating to twice that speed if necessary.

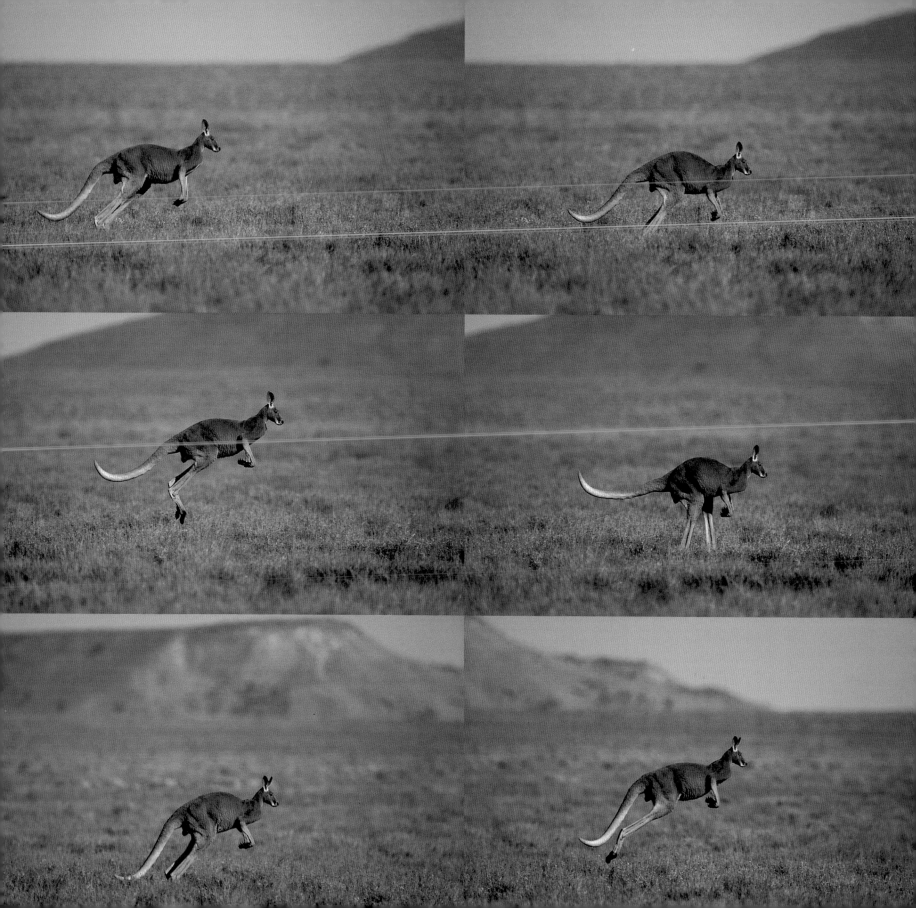

[l e f t]
At full stretch,
a kangaroo displays itself
as big as possible.

[r i g h t]
This kangaroo's forepaw
can barely reach the itch
on its back.

An eighteen-month-old kangaroo still has the soft and fluid contours of babyhood.

A young kangaroo nibbles on grass.

Clouds move in from the southwest. Rainfall is precious to this dry land.

A large male looks up from a moment of relaxation.

July mornings are shiveringly cold. In order to hold my camera I need to wear gloves. By noontime, however, the sun is so strong that on some days wearing even a T-shirt is too much. And when night falls, the temperature cools off again. Temperature differences between day and night are substantial because this is an inland desert region. Red kangaroos seem to handle cold better than heat. In the feeble light before sunrise, they are actively munching grass. Their round backs can barely be seen scattered amongst the grass.

Approaching wild kangaroos is very difficult. Cautious when approached, their big ears swivel around like radar. If they sense something in the air, they tense their whole bodies to their surroundings.

Reactions toward vehicles vary. Some red kangaroos begin running at the first sound of a motor vehicle. Others might see a car passing and simply turn slowly and hop away. While grazing, if one kangaroo should run, the rest will follow, scattering in different directions. They give the impression of being at once carefree and panicked.

Female red kangaroos are a bluish gray.

I proceed from Australia's eastern coast toward the west by way of the Great Dividing Range. The G.D.R. is a stretch of three-thousand-foot peaks. It is not particularly steep. As I traverse it heading west, spread out before me is an Australian outback totally different from the eastern approach.

The town of Broken Hill is located at the tip of the west end of New South Wales. It is about eight hundred miles from Sydney, the capital of New South Wales. Upon reaching this town, the reality of the outback is made plain.

Two hundred miles north of Broken Hill is Sturt National Park. The park is said to have the largest red kangaroo population in Australia. A 1991 study estimated some 1,002,000 kangaroos. The park is named for the English explorer Charles Sturt, who, in the mid 1800s, organized an expedition on the eastern coast to enter the ouback in search of an inland sea. The point where Sturt was thwarted by the desert and forced to give up is located in the northwest area of this park.

Sturt National Park is a severe environment for living things to survive in. It is an extremely dry desert region with eight inches or less annual precipitation. The sun shines incandescently. The ground is red, the sky is blue, and they meet at the horizon with a persistent monotonousness. Plants cover only patches of the ground.

As I watch a kangaroo standing straight up on its two hind legs along the ridge line of the red desert, I imagine its simple needs, and the difficulty of meeting those needs in this harsh land.

Kangaroos use their short upper limbs with great dexterity for eating, grooming, and fighting. They scratch themselves frequently; the tracks left by their sharp, pointed nails are visible in the furrows running across their red fur.

[l e f t   a n d   r i g h t]

Before settling down for a nap, a kangaroo scratches himself thoroughly .

In the early morning, after a night of rain, the
kangaroos gather in the valley. The ruddiness of
the male's bodies stands out vividly.

Two males box. Their fighting gradually
escalates to biting, throwing, and hurling
each other to the ground.

Kangaroo feces is pebbly and dry. After sniffing around the area, they drop their feces.

Kangaroos crowd around the water hole at dawn and dusk. Defenseless while drinking, the kangaroos are fraught with tension.

Kangaroos take delight in the sun. After sniffing around, a male, female, and young kangaroo

dig through the firm, pebble strewn sand and create shallow holes to rest in.

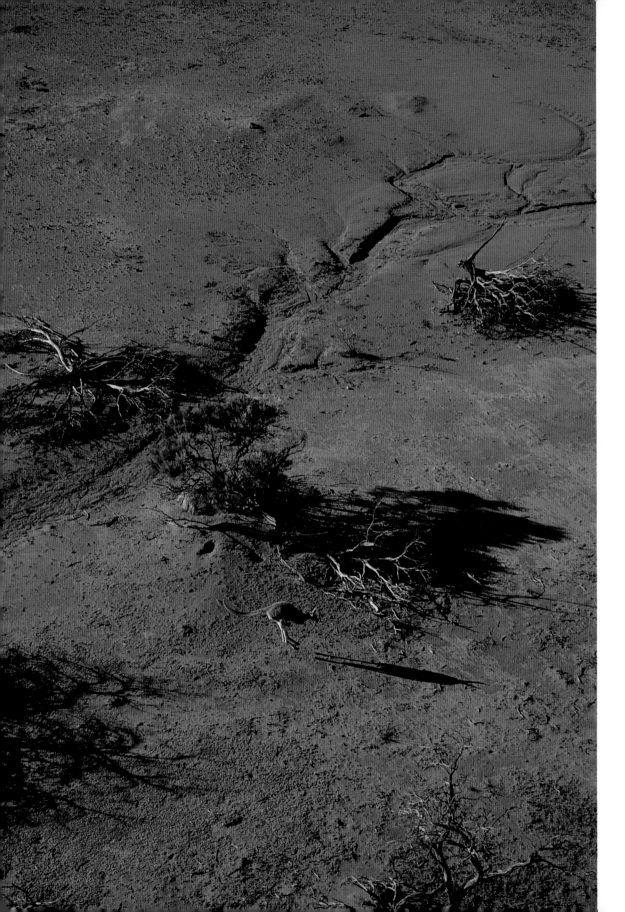

Meandering cracks like this one
will become a stream of water after
a rainfall.

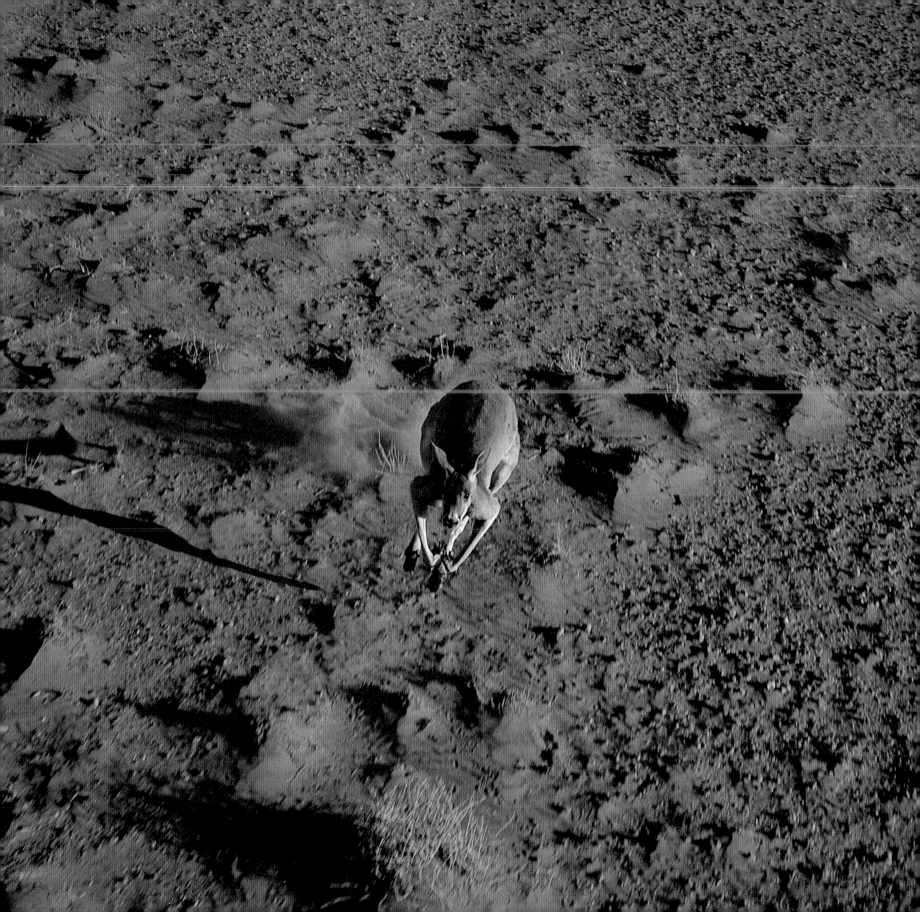

Flying in a helicopter, I observe this red kangaroo from the air. It is sometimes necessary to command a bird's-eye view in order to gain a different perspective on the land and its inhabitants. Mornings and evenings, the air currents are stable. Hazy with the sun's fire and clouds of sand, the horizon cuts the red ground from the blue sky along an easy curve.

I can clearly see many indentations here and there in the hard sand. Some are still in use by kangaroos at rest. Some of these impressions are in pairs, and their sizes vary.

From the air, the kangaroo looks unexpectedly white. When I see them on the ground, they seem redder. The powerful sunbeams reflecting off the red earth may visually deepen the red kangaroo's color.

The border with South Australia, west of Sturt National Park, is the Strzelecki Desert. Dunes line up toward the horizon. The morning sun shines onto them creating patterns of light and shadow. The color of the sand subtly changes and a green band can be seen along the top of the dunes. Remarkably, plants still live in this extremity.

Australia is the oldest of the seven continents. Its ancient strata can be seen clearly from the air and make me feel as if I am looking at the earth's skeleton.

After it rains, the typically hard earth becomes soft and muddy. Here, kangaroo tracks are visible in the ground. They will dry and remain like this until the next rain.

Australia celebrated its bicentennial in 1988. Over the course of its two-hundred-year history, much of the country consisted of large ranches.

For one hundred years, Sturt National Park was a sheep ranch. Because of continuous depredation, the land was devastated and sold off, and eventually turned into a national park. Today, the remains of the ranch can be seen here and there in the park. Among them are the reservoir tanks which are crucial to helping keep the park's animals alive. The tanks were originally dug as watering holes for grazing sheep. Some store rainwater, and some hold water pumped from underground by windmills.

The morning sun rises from the ruddy eastern horizon, immediately incandescent, and begins to glare. At the tank, shell parakeets, pink parakeets, moon-faced parakeets, and red kangaroos cautiously gather to drink. Rabbits, foxes, horses, camels, and dingoes, animals not indigenous to Australia, also come by to drink.

When the sun reaches its zenith, the tanks grow quiet. The animals take a break from drinking. The wind blows across the water surface of the red tank, and the ripples weave a netlike pattern. When the blurring red sun begins shining in the west, animals begin returning to the tank, and continue to come past midnight. Unless there is a severe drought, water is always available in the tanks.

Dingoes arrive after tracking the smell of a desiccated kangaroo corpse.

The intense rays of the sun dry out the body of a dead kangaroo. The average life span of a kangaroo is seven years.

Although wedge-tailed eagles and dingoes prey upon kangaroos, drought remains their biggest enemy.

A red kangaroo in a defensive stance with its eyes and ears alert to danger.

Kangaroos are generally tolerant of other animals. Chased by an emu, these kangaroos bound away.

Blue bushes pale under the morning sun. These kangaroos, too, look bleached. Both females, they are carrying large offspring in their pouches.

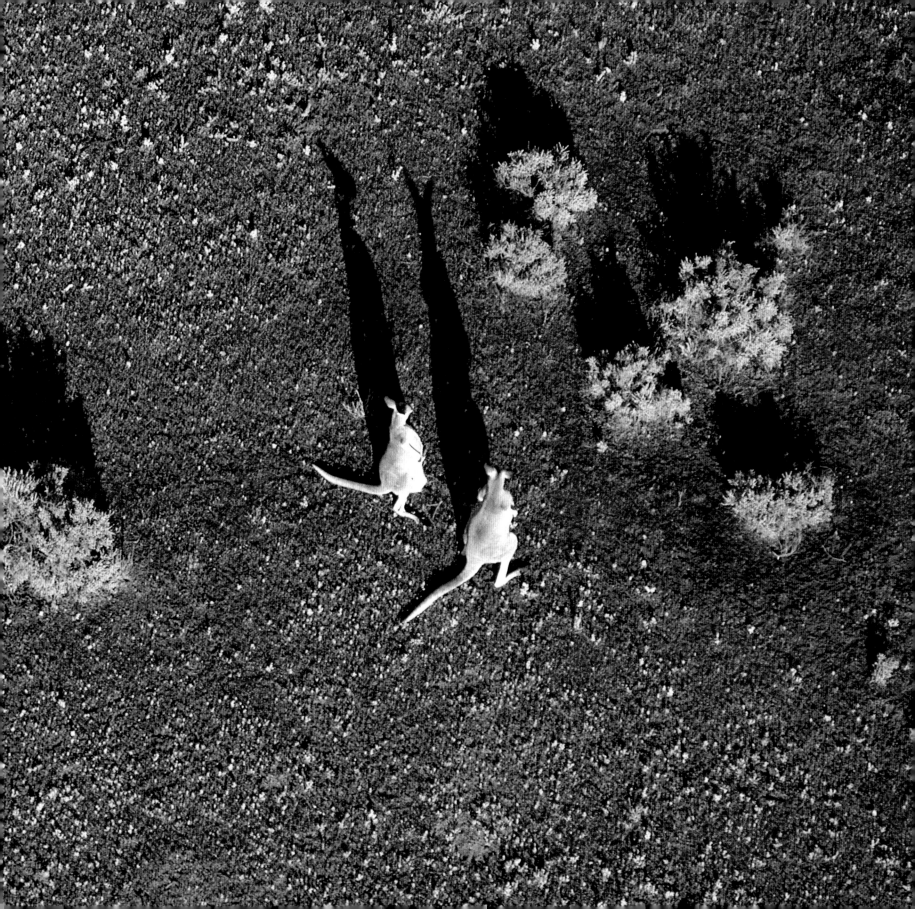

Using his strong tail for support, a male red
kangaroo stretches and displays his power to
everyone in his vicinity.

Two adult males box. The kangaroo on the right
is using his hind legs to kick its opponent. His tail
supports his roughly two-hundred-pound bulk.

A variety of phenomena can be found in the outback. Natural, man-made, or both, these phenomena are interconnected and have an effect on all the living things in the outback, including, of course, the red kangaroos. Take dust storms, for instance. Australians call them "instant nightfall"

One day, even though it was too early for twilight, a slight darkness drew up from the western horizon. A yellowish, cloudy, sandy color, it lay heavily over the sky and rapidly constricted our view. The wind began blowing hard. Our visibility shrank to a radius of about twenty-two yards. Nearby, wedge-tailed eagles perched in the treetops of eucalyptus trees. Although sitting on the trees' branches, the eagles were flapping their wings in the direction of the dust storm as if they were hovering. At the same time, some rabbits had been forced by the storm to crowd around the base of a tree. The movements of one of them caught the eye of one of the eagles. Immediately, the eagle took advantage of the opportunity, plunged down, and flew up holding one of the rabbits in its talons.

Wedge-tailed eagles are native to Australia. Rabbits, however, are non-indigenous. Now eagles and rabbits are linked together as predators and prey. After they were brought to Australia, the rabbits flourished throughout some one million two hundred square miles of land where they took up devouring the grass. Unlike cattle, rabbits eat not only the leaves but the roots as well. The land became devastated, and this is one of the causes of the outback's frequent dust storms.

A large red kangaroo male follows a female. He sniffs her scent while staying alert and cautious about his surroundings.

Red kangaroos do not have any particular reproductive season. The environment of the outback is severe, and reproduction is influenced by rainfall. Since they do not have any designated reproductive season, red kangaroos neither hold territory nor create harems.

A female red kangaroo is urinating. A male is attraced by the smell.

A male grabs a female by her tail with his forepaws. He slides his paws up her tail,
holds her by the waist, and they begin to copulate. Female red kangaroos reach breeding age
at approximately two years, males at approximately two-and-a-half years.

[u p p e r   l e f t]
While copulating, a male kangaroo rides the back of the female.

[b o t t o m   l e f t]
The female's back is soaked with the sweat of the male.

[r i g h t]
The female leaps up, but the male holds her waist tightly and does not let go.

In body color, male red kangaroos are red, and females are blue gray.

Males weigh about two hundred pounds and females about ninety pounds.

The Dingo Fence also serves as a state boundary. On this side is New South Wales, and on the other side is Queensland. Small groups of red kangaroos, called "mobs", may gather together when heading toward the same sources of food and water, but they do not form herds. Nomadic by nature, they sometimes range over two hundred miles searching for grass and water.

In the endlessly blue sky, which looks like a mantle of blue woolen cloth, a strand or two of cloud gently floats by. This is the most impressive sky in Australia, although I prefer to see a sky engorged by rain clouds.

In Sturt National Park's desert, rain is very unusual. One day it suddenly arrives—storming in from the Indian Ocean to the northwest in summer and in winter from the south and the Antarctic Ocean—capriciously pouring down.

On the morning of a rainy day, scattered clouds are strewn across the sky. The wind gradually shifts from the east to the north. Scattered clouds are blown by the wind and bunch up at the horizon. The clouds gradually become a slate blue wall, spreading over the sky, and bring rain.

This is the rain we have been eagerly waiting for. The red kangaroos hang their heads and round their backs. They react by putting their backs to the rain. It is a cold rain, and they shiver and stay still with their forepaws together. Joeys who were playing outside, seek shelter from the rain in their mothers' pouches. The kangaroos stoically endure the rain and try to preserve their physical energy as much as possible.

In the morning following the downpour, I pay a visit to one of the park's tanks. It's quiet—there is not a hint of life. Water pools are strewn throughout the park. The animals have scattered to sundry drinking areas to drink the water to their hearts' delight.

[u p p e r l e f t]

This infant is seven days old.

[m i d d l e l e f t]

It takes about thirty days for its nails to get some color. Its eyes are not yet open, however.

[b o t t o m l e f t]

By the hundredth day, its eyes are open.

[r i g h t]

At 130 days, a fine fur is growing all over its body.

Even after venturing out, a joey will continue to
stick its head into its mother's pouch to nurse.
It will continue to drink its mother's milk for
about four hundred days.

The time has come for this joey to stand on its own. Too big to be carried comfortably by its mother, it will never enter its mother's pouch again.

A mother passes saliva to her child.

A large joey climbs back into
its mother's pouch, magically disappearing
in a matter of moments.

This two-hundred-day-old juvenile is almost too big to fit into its mother's pouch.

A mother cleans her pouch by licking it thoroughly.

A mother enjoying a back scratch while her joey
rests awkwardly in her pouch.

An affectionate mother and child.

After a gestation period of approximately thirty-one days, red kangaroos are born as extremely under-developed infants weighing less than an ounce and measuring less than an inch long. Born from the urogenital opening, the newborn instinctively climbs up the front of its mother's pouch. Once it locates the pouch, it climbs in, clamps on to a teat, and will nurse for approximately 160 days before taking its first look at the outside world.

A female red kangaroo can nurse two children at once: a newborn who remains in her pouch and a young kangaroo who has left the pouch but who continues to nurse. At the same time, female red kangaroos have the amazing ability to store a dormant embryo in its womb and trigger its development or its disintegration depending on outside conditions. During times of extreme drought, for example, when grass is not widely available, red kangaroos will not reproduce.

As with all young animals, juvenile kangaroos are beguiling to watch. A kangaroo who has just left the pouch will remain close to its mother, exploring and frolicking but rarely straying far from her protection. If it does stray too far, it will rush headlong back to her safety.

A male and female red kangaroo bound along with a child between them. Male red kangaroos take no responsibility for raising their young. Although this trio looks like a family, they may just be a mother and child with an unrelated male tagging along.

A joey looks up at its mother, while a male leisurely grazes.

A male moves around to position himself in front of a female. The female stops grazing and returns his gaze.

My base camp for gathering material on the red kangaroo is in the only building left over from the sheep ranch that preceded Sturt National Park. It is made of wood and has a high floor that provides excellent ventilation in summer, giving both dryness and comfort. In winter, there is a bit too much ventilation! Power is supplied by a generator. To take a shower, I collect fallen trees, break them up, and heat the water with them.

Day to day tasks take up a fair amount of my time. I realize that I have slipped into outback time without knowing it and am at ease. Each locality has a rhythm that suits it. My tactic for collecting material is to adapt to wherever I am.

My camp is located about four miles from the border between New South Wales and Queensland. A part of this boundary is a fence known as the Dingo Fence. This side of the fence—the south side—is the park, and the other side—the north—is a ranch for sheep and cattle.

Dingoes are said to have come from Southeast Asia about five or six thousand years ago. In 1788, when the first Europeans came over to settle in Australia, the dingoes began to attack the ranchers' grazing cattle.

The Dingo Fence is a wire net fence that stands about six-and-a-half feet high and runs for about six thousand miles from South Australia to Queensland. It divides the south and the north and prevents dingoes from invading from the north to the south.

Despite the fence, dingoes often cross over. Serious problems have cropped up between the park and its neighboring ranches due to their conflicting purposes. Dingoes are the natural enemy of ranch livestock, and they are immediately shot. In the park, however, dingoes are wild animals and, although they are not given special protection, they are also not shot.

From the air, the Dingo Fence stands out oddly in the red desert. It makes me wonder about human beings trying to force nature to surrender.

An old male arrives at the periphery of a watering site. Standing still, he gazes around him.

A mother and child hop along in unison. When frightened, their leaps will fall out of sync.

[l e f t]
Even while grazing, kangaroos continue scratching.

[a b o v e]
A mother bounds across the plain with her child peering alertly from the pouch.

Sturt National Park's red kangaroo population is increasing. It is not simply a temporary rise—the increase shows itself as a gradual upward curve. However, once a drought hits, the population drops significantly. It is likely that the recent conditions suited the red kangaroo's reproduction pattern. Red kangaroos do not migrate when the season changes. They are nomadic, and range over the land searching for food and water.

I drive my car along the Dingo Fence. Due west, the dunes undulate like smooth waves with a few hundred yards distance between them. From the top of one of these dunes, I can see ahead young red kangaroos hopping in my direction along the fence. I stop the car and wait. The sun is above the rear of my vehicle. Seven young red kangaroos are headed my way, bobbing in and out of the dune waves. When they come to within twenty-two yards or so of the car, they finally see it and stop. They slam on their emergency brakes—their long hind legs—and their bodies tumble forward from the momentum. As I observe them and wonder what they will do, the red kanga-roos look at each other. After a while, one female starts to pass between the fence and the car. The others follow. As soon as the female approaches the rear of the car, she strikes the ground explosively with her hind legs. With this warning sound, she jumps back and inadvertently bumps against the fence at her side, creating panic among the other kangaroos. Unable to jump over the Dingo Fence, the seven young kangaroos scatter over the dunes, bounding away vigorously.

Tonight there is a full moon. I have always wanted to photograph the kangaroos at night. When I light them with the searchlight of my car, I realize that the red kangaroos are surprisingly near. Their eyes reflect red in the light. They seem to be less defensive at night.

The kangaroos are surprised at their own shadows dancing on the ground. Careful not to step over their own shadows, they try to escape by jumping so frenetically that they lose their balance and sway left and right attempting to stay upright.

At 4:00 a.m., the moon is white and still rides high in the sky. I would like to photograph the red kangaroos silhouetted against the rising sun, so I move my car to a place where red kangaroos often graze during the daytime. I turn off the car lights because they overpower my vision. The moon is still bright, and I soon begin to clearly make out my surroundings.

I wait for sunrise at a hillock from which I can see the horizon to the east. I put my VTR camera on a tripod mounted on my car door and put my 600-millimeter supertelescopic lens on it. Now, it is up to the kangaroos to come here just as the sun rises from the horizon.

But shooting this scene takes patience. For example, when the sun finally rises, the kangaroos might not be here. Or, even though they are here, they might not be in appropriate positions.

At sunrise, the wind starts to pick up. It shakes the car and vibrates even the supertelescopic lens, making it rattle. I had to get up at 4 a.m. for ten days in a row before getting the shot that I wanted.

Reflecting the car's headlights, the kangaroo's eyes look red.

Moonrise. The wind has died down and the creaking voice of insects can be heard in the eucalyptus woods.

Thanks to: Hideko Iwago; Australian Embassy; Broken Hill Tourist Information Center; BE-PAL; Australia-Japan Foundation; Shukan Asahi Weekly; NHK; NHK DBS; NHK Enterprises, Inc.; Mitsubishi Motors Corporation; Toyota Motor Corporation; New South Wales National Park Service; ICI Ishii Sports; Australian Tourist Commission.

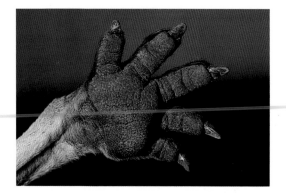

Forepaw of a male red kangaroo.

First published in the United States in 1994 by Chronicle Books.

First published in Japan in 1992 by Shogakukan, Inc.

Printed in Japan.

Library of Congress Cataloging in Publication Data
Iwago, Mitsuaki, 1950 -
    [Kangaroos]
    Mitsuaki Iwago's kangaroos / Mitsuaki Iwago.
          p.   cm.
    Translated from the Japanese.
    ISBN 0-8118-0785-1. — ISBN 0-8118-0760-6 (pbk.)
    1. Kangaroos. 2. Kangaroos—Pictorial works.   I. Title.
II. Title: Kangaroos.
QL737.M35I83   1994
599.2—dc20   93-49009
                           CIP

Translation: Michiko Shigaki and Thomas L. J. Daly
Editing (Japanese edition): Shuji Shimamoto
Text and cover design: Sarah Bolles

Distributed in Canada by
Raincoast Books
112 East Third Avenue
Vancouver, B.C. V5T 1C8

10 9 8 7 6 5 4 3 2 1

Chronicle Books
275 Fifth Street
San Francisco, California 94103